This bOOK Belongs to ... HERB

KT-233-308

WITHDRAWN

This book is dedicated to the very special Michael and Nora.

Thank You To
PAT. David.
bEn + Emily

7/12

Lis + JOBeY

ORCHARD BOOKS
First published in Great Britain in 2002
by Hodder Children's Books
This edition published in 2012
by the Watts Publishing Group

10 9 8 7 6 5 4 3

 A CIP catalogue record for this book
is available from the British Library.

ISBN 978 1 40830 772 4

Printed and bound in China

MIX
Paper from
responsible sources
FSC® C104740
FSC
www.fsc.org

Orchard Books
An imprint of Hachette Children's Group
Part of The Watts Publishing Group Limited
   Carmelite House, 50 Victoria Embankment,
      London EC4Y 0DZ

An Hachette UK Company
www.hachette.co.uk
www.hachettechildrens.co.uk

Who's Afraid of The Big Bad Book?

Lauren Child

ORCHARD

Herb loved storybooks.

Although he wasn't a very good reader, it didn't matter because he could tell a lot from the pictures. Herb liked the scary ones best with pictures of dinosaurs gobbling up other dinosaurs, or swooping vampires chasing people who had foolishly decided to go for a midnight stroll without any garlic.

Herb read his books everywhere. This was why many of the pages were stickily stuck together, soggy round the edges and usually had bits of banana, biscuit and the odd pea squashed between the pages.

On this particular night,
Herb's friend Ezzie was staying over.
Earlier, the two of them had been playing
a game, involving a great deal of
untidying things

and,

by the evening,

Herb

had trouble even finding his bed.

By the time he had, Ezzie was already slightly snoring.
So Herb searched around for a book to amuse him until he
dozed off but the only one he managed to find was
a book of **fairy tales.**

It hadn't been looked at in a very long time and was quite dusty.
It was actually quite exciting but even so Herb's eyes soon
became **heavy** and, before he could close the book,

he fell asleep with his head on the page.

Herb woke with a start to hear a strange high-pitched shrieking noise. He looked over to see if Ezzie was awake but there was no sign of him at all. Furthermore, his bed had become sort of lumpy and huge, which was funny because Herb had always found his bed to be just right.

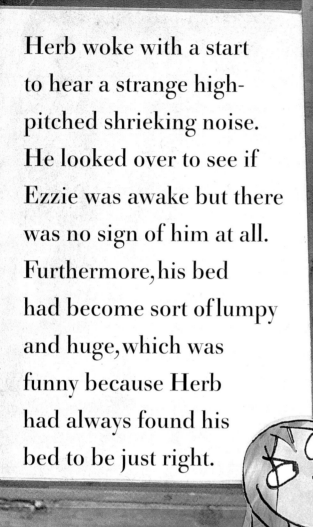

'WHAT ARE YOU DOING HERE? HOW DARE YOU BE ON THIS PAGE? I AM THE STAR AND I SAY YOU ARE NOT ALLOWED IN THIS STORY!' shrieked the shrieking thing.

'Wwwhere am I?' stammered Herb.

'ON MY PAGE!' screeched the girl.

'But who are you?' asked Herb, not sure that he wanted to know. 'I,' said the little girl, somehow managing to raise her voice even higher,

Herb scrabbled out of the bed as fast as he could, scooted down the stairs and went … *slap, bang, wallop!* … into three differently-sized bears.

'Whoops! I'm so sorry,' squeaked Herb terrified. 'I didn't mean to be here.'

'Oh, that's quite all right,' said the largest bear. 'It could happen to anyone.'

'And does all the time,' said the small bear, scowling at Goldilocks.

Bananas about bananas!

'*Ahem, hem!*'
coughed Goldilocks.
'IN CASE YOU PEA BRAINS
HAVE FORGOTTEN, THIS
STORY IS CALLED
"GOLDILOCKS AND
THE THREE BEARS"
NOT "THE LITTLE
SHOW-OFF IN
PYJAMAS HAS
BREAKFAST!"'

'How about some porridge?'
said the medium-sized bear.

'You might find it
too hot or too cold.

I'm afraid we're
out of just right.'

*Herb ran
for it!*

He ran past two children nibbling a house made of ginger biscuits. 'I wouldn't do that!' called Herb. 'Oh, get lost!' shouted the children.

He ran past a man climbing up what looked like a long plait of hair. **'Ouch!'** cried the voice belonging to the hair.

Herb ran all the way

There seemed to be a party going on.

Everyone was dressed up to the nines and dancing in wigs. One by one the dancers noticed Herb and the music ground slowly to a halt. It was so quiet you could hear a pea drop or was it a pin? Well, you could have heard something drop had it not been for the couple in crowns having a furious discussion in loud voices.

'Where the dickens is that twerp Prince Charming?'

'Never mind him. Where the devil is my throne?'

Herb couldn't help noticing that the queen had a moustache drawn on in biro!

And when he saw a cat wearing a feathered hat and high-heeled boots, Herb ran a bit faster.

through the forest...

AT LONG LAST, HE CAME TO AN ENORMOUS DOOR. IT WAS DIFFICULT TO OPEN BECAUSE THE ILLUSTRATOR HAD DRAWN THE HANDLE MUCH TOO HIGH UP BUT, AFTER THREE ATTEMPTS AT JUMPING, HERB MANAGED TO GRAB IT AND SLOWLY CREAK THE DOOR OPEN.

'And who might you be?' demanded he queen. 'This is a ivate Royal party ou know, no one in yjamas is invited.'

m Herb,' said Herb. 'I own this book.'

so you're the doodler o ruined my looks,' she said, pointing at her moustache. 'And where's my throne, you... ou scissor-snipper!'

It was then that Herb remembered. Last year, when he was much, much younger, he had drawn moustaches and glasses on many of his book characters and added telephones to all of the rooms. He had been going through a scribbling phase. He had also cut out the royal thrones for a model spaceship that he and Ezzie were making. And, he had a horrible feeling that he might be responsible for the disappearance of Prince Charming ...

As Herb wondered desperately what to do next, he noticed his
pencil case lying on the floor; he'd been looking for it for months.
'It's all right, I can draw you a new throne,' he said.
'*Make sure it's got lots of twirly bits,*' blustered the king.
'*And I want it gold, of course,*' ordered the queen.
Herb didn't have a gold crayon; it would have to be green.
The queen did not look impressed.
Then, finding the eraser, Herb started to rub away at the queen's moustache.

'*Ow, ow, OW! That really hurts!*
Seize him!' she roared.

Herb made a dash for it.

There wasn't time to get to the door but, by snipping a hole in the
palace floor, Herb managed to wriggle through onto the next page.
He could hear the queen shouting, '*Look, he's at it again!*'

Herb found himself in an oddly arranged room.

'Who are you? You measly little rodent.'

Looking up, Herb saw Cinderella's wickedly mean stepmother and her ugly daughters.

'I'm Herb,' called Herb. 'What are you doing up there?'

'I wonder… are we pretending to be flies…?' scoffed the woman, 'or could it be that some some vile good-for-nothing child tore out our page and put it back upside down?'

'I wonder who would do that?' said Herb, slightly blushing.

'Probably some hideous little boy,'

snarled the stepmother, fixing Herb with her beady eyes.

'Now we can't get
to the ball and
Prince Charming can't
fall madly, utterly in
love with us. It's
so unfair,'
whined the pudgy sister.

'He wouldn't look twice at you,'
snapped the skinny one.

'Oh do be quiet,'
hissed the stepmother.
'I'm feeling queasy.'

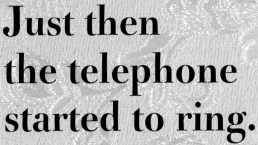

Just then the telephone started to ring.

Sticking telephones in fairy tales had seemed funny at the time, but Herb could see that they could turn out to be rather a nuisance.

'Hello? Why hello your majesty ...

Yesss ... as a matter of fact there is a little

pyjamared boy here. He did what? ... Oh he did,

did he? Don't worry, I'll deal with the little

weasel,' she said, giving Herb a shrivelling look.

'Oh, and by the way, if you see that nosy Goldilocks

brat tell her to bring a ladder over.'

'So this is your doing!'

she screamed, leaping onto her chair.

'I'm going to make
you wish you'd never
opened a book!'

Herb speedily drew a
door on the wall, ran through it
and slammed it shut.

'Come back here
you little
horror!'

she screeched.

Herb was in a very dusty kitchen. His feet were sticking to the floor and there were what looked like giant biscuit crumbs stuck all over the place.

'Sorry about the dirt,' said a bedraggled-yet-pretty girl.

'Aren't you meant to be at the royal ball?' asked Herb.

'Yes, but I had to come home because the prince, achoo..., was late and my party dress dissolved into rags and I really looked, achoo..., a mess and then my carriage turned back into a pumpkin, which was sort of embarrassing. Would you like a cup of, achoo..., tea?'

She really was very nice and Herb was beginning to feel extremely guilty,

because he had just remembered where Prince Charming was:

Herb had cut him out to make a birthday card for his mother.

'If only I could get out of this book I could find the prince for you,' he said.

'Ooh... I know who can help,' said Cinderella,

picking up her phone.

'Drat! Absolutely maddening! I was just in the middle of a spell. This had better be important!'

'It's an emergency! Absolutely everybody's after me.

You have to help me get out of this book!' yelled Herb.

'Well let me see...

A. Are you my fairy godchild?

No, you are not. I don't do boys; only girls worst luck.

B. What do you expect when you go about scribbling and snippering and generally causing mayhem?

This is no way to treat a book you know!

And C...

jumping into other people's stories, really is very rude.'

'But I can't find my way out,' pleaded Herb, near his wits' end.

'All right, all right, keep your pyjamas on. I suppose I'll have to come to the rescue as always. Now where did I put my wand?'

At that moment
the door flew open.

'HE'S IN YOUR KITCHEN,
LOOKING FOR
MORE FOOD!'

It was the
unmistakably
ear-piercing voice of
Goldilocks. Right behind
her was the wicked stepmother
and she was not in a pretty mood,
having snagged her stockings
climbing a ladder out of the
upside-down room.

'What shall I do?' flustered Herb.

'Quick! Climb up the text!' said the fairy godmother.

Herb grabbed hold of the letters and scrabbled up the sentences. Some of the words were a bit *weak* and the whole lot started to wobble.

... screamed Goldilocks so loudly that the whole book shook and slipped off the bed, sending Herb falling headlong through the air onto ...

. . . his own bedroom floor.

'Wh-what's happening?' squeaked a startled Ezzie, sitting bolt upright in bed. As you can imagine it all took some explaining.

Ezzie and Herb spent the rest of the night putting the storybook back to rights: rubbing out moustaches cleaning out crumbs and blowing away dust. The bewildered Prince Charming was prised off the birthday card and sticky-taped back into the ballroom. His dancing would never quite be the same again due to severe leg creasing.

It was tempting to leave the wicked stepmother's room upside-down, but Herb resisted. However, he just couldn't help drawing a padlock on the three bears' front door. And Ezzie just couldn't help sticking a wig on Goldilocks. Well, serves her right for being such a meany.

...and they all lived happily ever after

The End

So, the next time Herb opened the book, he saw
a little girl standing outside the three bears' cottage
desperately trying to open the door —

a very cross little girl with mousey brown hair.